LITTLE
GREEN
DONKEY

ANUSKA ALLEPUZ

For my Dad

WALKER BOOKS
AND SUBSIDIARIES
LONDON · BOSTON · SYDNEY · AUCKLAND

First published 2019 by Walker Books Ltd, 87 Vauxhall Walk, London SE11 5HJ • © 2019 Anuska Allepuz • The right of Anuska Allepuz to be identified as author/illustrator of this work has been asserted by her in accordance with the Copyright, Designs and Patents Act 1988 • This book has been typeset in Didact Gothic • Printed in China • All rights reserved. No part of this book may be reproduced, transmitted or stored in an information retrieval system in any form or by any means, graphic, electronic or mechanical, including photocopying, taping and recording, without prior written permission from the publisher • British Library Cataloguing in Publication Data: a catalogue record for this book is available from the British Library • ISBN 978-1-4063-8466-6 • www.walker.co.uk • 10 9 8 7 6 5 4 3 2 1

Hello there! I'm Little Donkey.
And I love eating grass.
Grass is my absolute favourite.

My mum is always trying to get me to eat other food.
"Little Donkey, *please* have a little,
tiny taste!" she says.

"No, thanks," I say.
A life of eating grass,
is just fine for me.

Grass is just so juicy
and zingy, so sweet
and tangy – what
flavoury fresh greenness!

My pillow is made of grass,
so that when I wake up,
I can start eating it right away.

I really am the happiest
little donkey when my tummy
is full of grass.

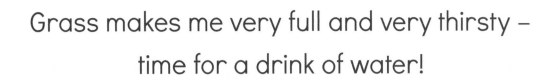

Grass makes me very full and very thirsty –
time for a drink of water!

Ooh, ooh, grass you are so greeeeen,
In the sun, you have a sheeeeen,
I like to eat you day and night,
Just give me one more juicy bite!

What has happened?
Is that ME?

Am I ... GREEN?

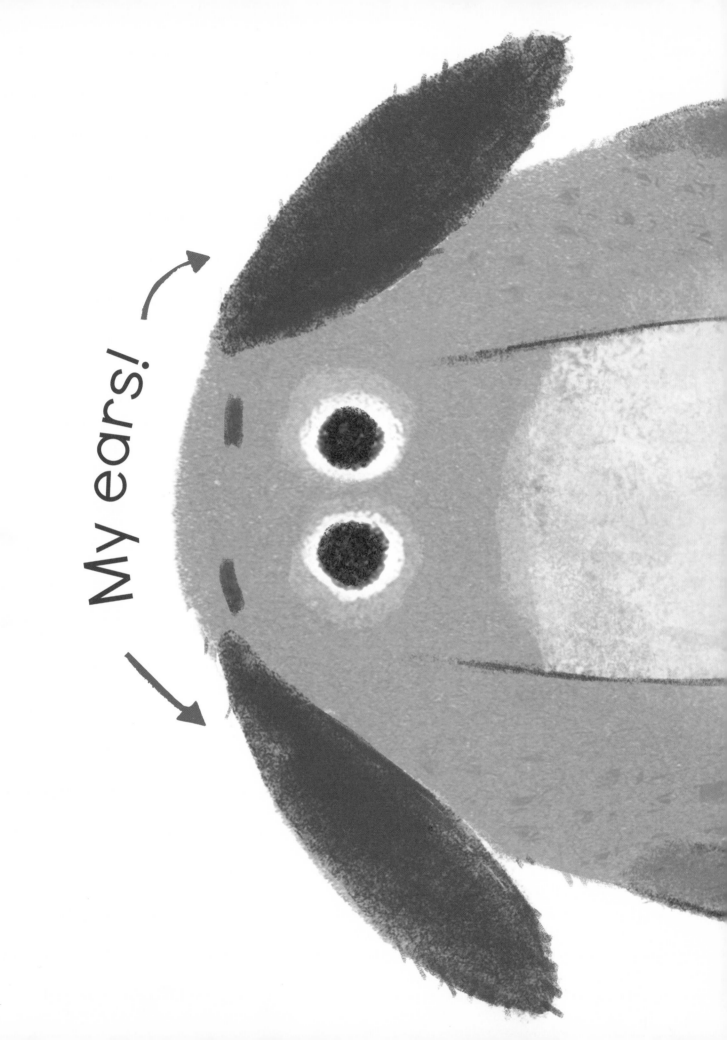

My ears!

My legs!

My tummy!

My arms!

My tail!

They're ALL GREEN!

I am a GIGANTIC herb.

Oh no! My mum will find out that
I have eaten TOO much grass...
What can I do?

Aha! This mud
will hide the green.

And these leaves
will help.

Yes, nobody will *ever* guess...
I'm a genius.

"Little Donkey! You're all GREEN!" says Mum.
"You have finally eaten too much grass.

It's really time to try and eat some new food.
I bet you'll like them just as much
as grass," she says.

I'm not convinced there's anything more delicious than grass...

BLEUGH.

Oranges are too juicy.

PEW! PEW!

Watermelon is full of seeds!

URRRR.

Broccoli is ... too *green*.

YUCK!
Apples ... no, thank you.

Grapeeees... PFFFT.

Carrots.
Hmmmm.
Carrots are ...

SO DELICIOUS!

Such orangey, crunchy,
crispy AMAZINGNESS.
Mmmmmmm...
Carrots are my favourite!

Carrots make me very full and very thirsty –
time for a drink of water!

Carrots, you are so cruuuunchy!
Carrots make me feel so muuuunchy!
Carrots for breakfast, carrots for tea,
Carrots, oh carrots, are all I can seeeee!

Great.

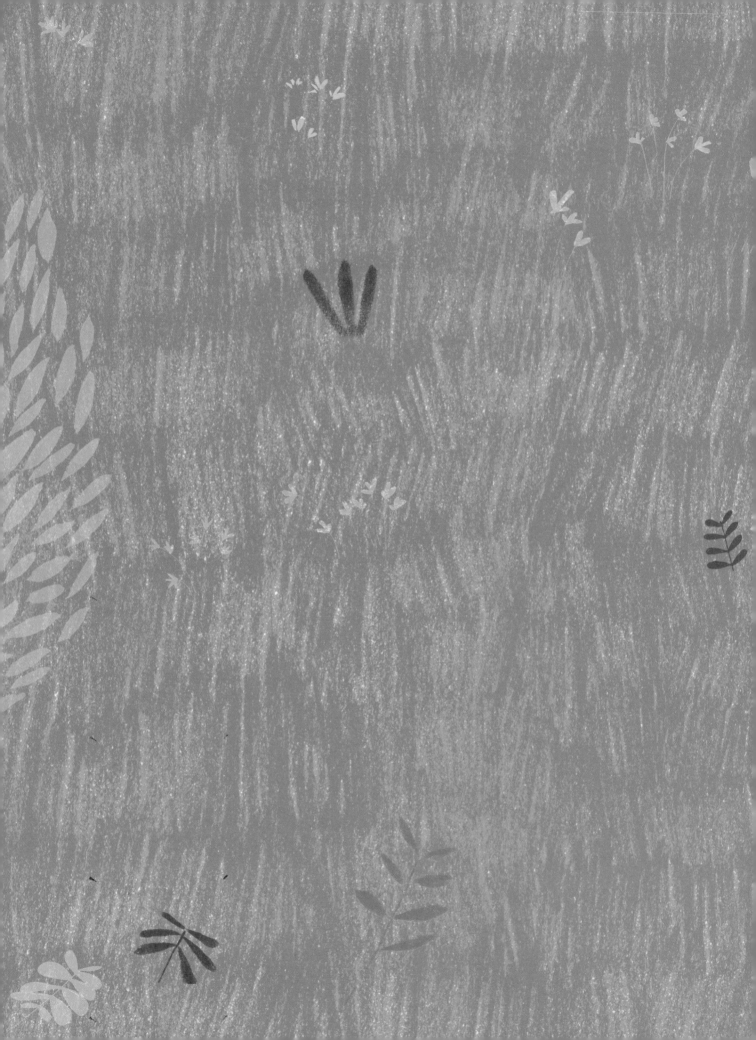